Pound Puppies

Lovable, Huggable

Lost and Found

By Teddy Slater
Illustrated by Pat Paris

A GOLDEN BOOK • NEW YORK
Western Publishing Company, Inc., Racine, Wisconsin 53404

Paul Peterson, his parents, and their dog, Sugar, had just spent a wonderful weekend at a cozy country inn. But now it was time to start the long trip back home—and Sugar was missing! Mr. Peterson whistled, Paul wailed, but Sugar didn't appear.

The family searched high and low, but they still couldn't find Sugar. When night finally fell, the Petersons had to give up and leave without her.

Before they left, they told the innkeeper to keep an eye out for Sugar, and they reported the lost dog to the local pound. They also hung up signs all over town offering a big reward for Sugar's return.

Paul cried all the way home.

"Don't cry," his dad said. "Someone will find Sugar."

Back home, Paul eagerly awaited news of his dog. But days and then weeks went by without a word. Poor Paul had no way of knowing that Sugar was really on her way home.

In fact, she was practically in her own backyard...

when dogcatcher Dabney Nabbit scooped her up and took her to the Pound. It was clear to Nabbit that this well-dressed dog belonged to someone, but he had no idea who that someone might be. Somewhere during Sugar's trip home she had lost her I.D. collar.

Sugar's journey had been a long and hard one. By the time Nabbit nabbed her, Sugar was a little bit sick and a whole lot tired and hungry.

Supervisor Bigelow wasted no time checking Sugar in at the Pound. After some quick pawprinting, she was off to see the vet.

Doc Weston took one look at the tired pup and put her straight to bed.

"All you need is some tender loving care and a good night's sleep," the kindly vet said to Sugar. "You'll feel better in the morning."

But Sugar still felt weak and worried when she awoke the next morning. She perked up, though, when Doc Weston brought her some visitors—Cooler, Nose Marie, and the rest of the Pound Puppies.

The Pound Puppies introduced themselves. Then Cooler asked, "What's a cute pup like you doing in a place like this?"

LOST

After Sugar told her sad tale, Doc announced that visiting hours were over. "This pooch is still a little sick," she said. "She needs her rest."

So Cooler and his friends left, but not before they'd promised to reunite Sugar with her family.

Later that morning Barkerville said to Cooler, "According to my maps, the Petersons live three blocks from here. We'll have that pup home in no time."

"Not so fast," Nose Marie said. "Don't forget what Doc said. Sugar's still too sick to travel. We can't have her wandering around in the snow."

"Well," said Cooler, "if we can't get Sugar to the Petersons, I have a plan to bring them here."

After Cooler had explained his idea, the Pound Puppies sneaked back into Sugar's room. Her eyes lit up with hope as Cooler spoke, but they dimmed just as quickly when he got to the part about unraveling her sweater.

"Mrs. Peterson knitted this just for me," Sugar protested.

"It's only a bunch of wool," Cooler pointed out. "She'll make you a new one once you're home safe and sound."

As soon as Sugar agreed the Pound Puppies began working on the first step of their plan. Within minutes Sugar's beautiful sweater had been turned back into a ball of shocking pink yarn. Then Nose Marie twisted the yarn into a thick coil.

The second step of Cooler's plan went off without a hitch. Scrounger had no problem hiding himself in a trash can. And when the trash was taken out a little later, Scrounger was taken out with it!

Once he was outside, Scrounger reached into the trash can, pulled out a few half-chewed bones, and tossed them over the Pound fence. That's all it took to distract Itchey and Snitchey from their guard duty. While the two guard dogs munched greedily on the bones, Scrounger opened the gate, and Cooler and Barkerville strolled out, unwatched. As they did Scrounger calmly walked back in.

Now it was time for the third and final step of the plan. Cooler tied one end of the pink yarn around a streetlamp in front of the Pound. Barkerville checked his maps once more, then started off for the Petersons' house. Cooler followed behind, looping the brightly colored yarn around tree trunks and fence posts along the way.

When they reached the Petersons' house, Cooler spied a shiny green bike on the front porch. "This must be Paul's," he said, tying a big pink bow around the handlebars. "That bow ought to catch his attention," Cooler said happily before he and Barkerville returned to the Pound.

"Mission accomplished!" Cooler told the rest of the Pound Puppies, who had been waiting anxiously to hear how things went.

"And now we'd better get some sleep," Barkerville said. "I have a feeling tomorrow's going to be a big day."

All the Pound Puppies fell asleep with big smiles on their faces.

When Paul went out to play the next morning, he could hardly believe his eyes. The pink yarn was the exact same color as Sugar's sweater. Paul was sure that Sugar was nearby.

"Mom! Dad! Come out and look. Sugar must be around here somewhere. She left part of her sweater on our porch!" Paul shouted gleefully.

Paul's parents didn't share his excitement, though. "It's just a coincidence," Mrs. Peterson said. "There must be lots of pink wool around."

Mr. Peterson nodded in agreement. Of course, neither of them could explain exactly what the pink bow was doing on Paul's bike.

"Maybe one of your friends did it as a joke," Mr. Peterson suggested.

But Paul was already dashing down the porch stairs to see where the yarn led. His parents had no choice but to run after him. All three Petersons followed the pink trail down the driveway, up the block, around the corner, across the street—and right to the Pound.

"It *is* Sugar's sweater!" Paul cried when he realized where they were. "She must be inside."

Paul marched up the stairs and walked right over to
Supervisor Bigelow's desk. He held out a picture of Sugar
and said, "This is my dog, Sugar. Is she here?"

"She certainly looks familiar," Bigelow said. "Why don't
we take a look around." He led Paul and his parents to the
vet's office.

The Petersons found Sugar sitting up in bed, looking almost as good as new. Doc decided that the best medicine Sugar could have was the love of her family. Paul wrapped her up, warm and snug.

Cooler and the gang were sad to see their new friend go, but they were glad to know that Sugar was on her way home. After all, finding homes for lost and stray dogs is what Pound Puppies are all about.